The First Church of Pete's Garage

by Paul McCusker

Baker's Plays
7611 Sunset Blvd.
Los Angeles, CA 90042
bakersplays.com

DEDICATION . .
For Mike Marmen. For Many Reasons.

The First Church of Pete's Garage was premiered August 27, 1982 at Grace Baptist Church in Bowie, Maryland The original cast consisted of Mike Marmen, Kelly Gibbs, David Hoff, Rick Davis, Steve Smith, John Dunlap, Eric Kruhm, Ken Pape, Donna Tate, Debbie Byrd, Mac Ward Sr , Beth Vass and Mac Ward, Jr Special love and thanks to all of them

– Paul

CAST OF CHARACTERS

PETE—*The idealistic young man who believes he can start a perfect church.*

MARY—*Pete's girlfriend. She's extremely skeptical about the whole idea and not very thrilled about her possible place in it*

DAN—*Pete's long suffering friend and "secretary"*

TERRY—*Tries to stay practical and logical amidst this obvious insanity*

JIM—*He sees opportunity in their new church personal opportunity*

FRED—*He has a very "object"-ive attitude about the church plus some ideas of his own on its outreaches.*

RALPH—*One of the members who thinks about food a lot   and reaches out to others who think like him.*

CHRIS—*Only motivation is to get home to do homework*

LESLIE—*She wants to direct the choir*

ANN—*She wants to direct the choir, too*

WALLY—*He's a dirty, smelly bum Ralph brings in off the street (literally)*

THE PASTOR—*A voice unseen   . but very wise and understanding.*

FOUR "INTERVIEWERS"—*Four extras (or they could be played by Terry, Fred, Ralph and Chris) in the audience.*

STAGING

Except where noted, all action takes place in Pete's garage.

PRODUCTION NOTES

This one-act should be extremely easy to stage and execute. Whether you're using a curtain and lights, one or the other, you shouldn't have any problems adapting this to your particular stage situation. All action (except at the beginning and end) takes place in Pete's garage. Outside of that, scenes can be done in front of a curtain or isolated with a spotlight. Feel free to be creative and imaginative in any way that will work best with your audience.

Because churches (and its members) vary in so many different ways, two of the characters have been written so that they may be played by either sex (Terry and Chris). Hopefully, it will help you in your casting.

Pete's garage should, obviously, look like a garage. Except for a table and chairs (for the business meeting), it should have just what most garages would have . . . . namely: trash cans, tools, shovels, rakes, paint cans, boxes, an assortment of containers, saw horse . . . etc., etc. (you can model it after your own garage if you like). The table can be placed Center Stage or towards Stage Right (just off-center).

THE FIRST CHURCH OF PETE'S GARAGE

Scene One

Spotlight (or in front of curtain) comes up on the cast crowded together center stage. They are facing the audience but actually looking at a specific point above them. Everyone is looking nervous and anxious except Peter (who looks more resolved and assured). They are standing in the Pastor's office. As we join them, Pete is just wrapping up his discourse on problems in the church, its people and its administration. As spokesman for the youth group, he felt it was their duty to confront the Pastor. The Pastor is not seen. He is a voice .. warm, compassionate, understanding and indulgent of the whims of these young people.

PETE. (*Speaking in conclusion*) . . . . and that's how I, er, *we* feel.

PASTOR. So you think the church has problems.

PETE. Yes, Pastor, and we thought it was time to let you know. We believe . . . (*Looks around to the group for encouragement*) . . . well, we believe that our church just isn't the way Christ intended the church to be. There's so much bickering, backstabbing, gossip and pettiness . . . everyone's divided over doctrine and nobody seems to

be living a fruitful, abundant life. I think Christ expected
more. He wants us to love one another and be unified.
We don't see that here This place seems spiritually
stagnant.

PASTOR. (*Thoughtfully*) Hmmmmmm .. and you think
you can do better

PETE (*Caught off guard*) Do better? (*Looks around to
the group*) Can we? (*They all look away, unsure and un-
willing to make a commitment Pete speaks suddenly, with
conviction*) Yes I think we can. (*The group looks at him
with surprise as he looks back to the Pastor*) Yes! I think
we're young enough and open-minded enough to do it
and do it right

PASTOR. Okay Let's try an experiment. (*Pause*) Go
start your own church

EVERYONE (*Except Pete*) What?

PETE. You want us to start our own *church*?

PASTOR Yes. If this church isn't meeting your spiritual
needs and you think you can do better, start one of your
own.

PETE (*Pondering the idea*) Start our own church

TERRY But how?

LESLIE Where will we meet?

ANN Who'll be our Pastor?

PASTOR. *You'll* have to work that out

FRED. It's impossible.

PASTOR. It wasn't for us when we started *this* church
(*Tongue in cheek*) That is, *before* we became stagnant

PETE. (*Brightening*) We'll do it!

EVERYONE. What?

PETE Yes! We can do it. We can start by meeting in
my garage! It's a *great* idea! (*Everyone looks at him puzzled and with doubt. Pete looks back to the Pastor and speaks*

enthusiastically) Pastor, you've got yourself an experiment! (*BLACKOUT*)

Scene Two

Lights (curtain) up on the full stage   Pete's garage   Pete and Mary enter mid-conversation carrying papers to be distributed around the table (which can be done during the dialogue)

PETE. Okay, okay, I know you don't like the idea but it's a *challenge* It's an opportunity to start from scratch and make a church the way Christ wanted it (*Drops everything on the table*) Besides, it's a chance to show the adults at the church that we're not just a bunch of idiot kids like they think (*He begins straightening the room up for the meeting*)

MARY And you think the adults at the church are overwhelmed with respect for us because of this? They're probably laughing hysterically.

PETE. Let them laugh. We'll show them

MARY Pride goeth before the fall. (*Pauses, speaks hesitantly*) And what about us?

PETE Who us?

MARY What are *we* going to do?

PETE Which *we*, Mary? We the people, we the church, we the youth group?

MARY. Will you stop thinking in mass groupings for a moment. *We! Us!* You and me!

PETE. What about we, I mean, us?

MARY. I don't know if I'm meant to be a Pastor's girlfriend.

PETE. Hold on now . . . who said you'll be a Pastor's girlfriend? Nobody said I'm the Pastor.

MARY. You will be. Nobody else would be crazy enough to want it.

PETE. We won't know until we vote on it.

MARY. Don't be silly. We know now. You'll be elected and I'll be a Pastor's girlfriend. And everyone will expect me to act a certain way and do certain things.

PETE. What are you talking about?

MARY. Oh, Pete, you know. I'll have to dress up all the time in case someone decides to come by and counsel with me. I'll have to lead Bible studies and know everything there is to know about scriptures. I'll have to sing in the choir, visit the sick people in the hospital, organize socials, bake cookies, cheer you up when you're down, (*Pete listens to this with mounting amazement — he slowly sinks into a chair*) smile all the time even when I don't want to and I'll have to listen to the *same* people complain about the *same* problems and give them the *same* advice over and over again. Not to mention typing church bulletins, a newsletter, organizing a ladies auxiliary, keeping the nursery and probably cleaning up the church bathroom! And that's only the *half* of it!

PETE. (*Shocked*) Is *that* what a Pastor's girlfriend does?

MARY. You bet your pulpit! And it would be *worse* if we got married!

PETE. (*Dumbfounded*) Wow. (*Frowns*) But what does that leave for the Pastor to do?

MARY. Not much. That's why I think you should give this whole silly idea up. Let's go back to the *real* church and forget all this.

PETE. (*Still dumbfounded for a moment, then snaps out of it*) No, Mary, we can't. The Pastor dared us. It would be wrong to give up already without even trying.

MARY. I think you're biting off more than you can chew. I don't think you realize what you're getting into.

PETE. But that's where the challenge is! (*Stands boldly*) Did Columbus know when he first set sail? Did the Pilgrims know when they landed on Chrysler Rock?

MARY. *Plymouth* Rock. (*One by one, Dan, Ralph, Terry, Chris, Jim and Fred enter as PETE speaks the following*)

PETE. Same difference. (*Continuing*) Did our patriotic forefathers pause to wonder as they drafted and signed the Declaration of Independence? (*As he speaks — becoming more impassioned — everyone, but Mary, begins humming "America The Beautiful" as they enter They should hum softly at first then louder as Pete gets more excited in his delivery. They should stand in a line behind him and time it so that his speech ends just as they break into the chorus*) Did Washington know that freezing winter at Valley Forge? Did Lewis and Clark know when they first set their canoes in foreign streams? (*More excited, he stands on a chair*) Did the Pioneers know when they ventured across the vast unchartered expanse of land? (*Humming gets louder*) Did Edison or Bell know as they experimented with unknown forces? (*He gets louder, even more dramatic, so does humming*) Did Admiral Byrd know when he first set foot on the North Pole? Did the Astronauts have any idea when they said "One small step for men, one giant leap for mankind"!?!?!?

EVERYONE. (*Singing now in unison with hands over hearts. Pete places his hand over heart and looks ahead gallantly*) "America, America, God shed His grace on thee. And crown thy good with brotherhood from sea to shining sea!"

PETE. (*Climbing down off chair, speaking to the still*

skeptical Mary) See?

MARY You forgot a question.

PETE. Oh?

MARY. Yes. Did the Captain of the Titanic know to look for icebergs? Bye. *(She exits Stage Left)*

PETE Okay. Let's get on with our business meeting. *(Everyone sits down at the table preferably, from left to right TERRY, CHRIS, RALPH, PETE, DAN, JIM and FRED Be sure no one's back is to the audience)*

TERRY. The first thing we should discuss is—

PETE Hold it, Terry. The Bible says to do everything decently and in order. We're going to run this meeting according to rules

TERRY. What rules?

PETE. We'll do this according to rules set up in the Penitentiary Procedures.

DAN. Parliamentary.

PETE What?

DAN *Parliamentary,* not "penitentiary."

PETE Oh.

TERRY. What are those?

PETE. Well, they're . . . they're . . . well, they're rules to make sure everything is done decently and in order. Dan agreed to be our minute taker.

TERRY. This is ridiculous. *What* did you call him?

PETE A minute taker.

TERRY. *(Meant to ridicule)* You mean secretary.

DAN. *(Stands offended)* I am not!

TERRY. *(Challenging him)* Then what do you call it?

DAN. *(At a loss)* I'm a . . . . well, ah . . . *(Suddenly)* a minuteman! *(Sits back down, pleased with himself but puzzled)*

TERRY. *(Stands)* I've heard enough. Meeting's adjourned. (*Begins to walk away*)

PETE. (*Pleading*) Wait, Terry. Come on, give it a chance We'll do it this way now until we get settled *Then* we can change it if we want. This is just a way to keep things from getting too confusing (*Pauses, motions to chair*) Please?

TERRY. Oh, okay. (*Sits back down*)

CHRIS. (*Impatiently*) Can we get on with this? I have tons of homework to do

PETE. All right, Dan, what do we do first?

DAN. Take roll call. (*Everyone looks around at each other*)

CHRIS I think everyone's here

PETE. No. We have to do this right Go on, Dan.

DAN. Please give me an appropriate response when I call your name . . Ralph (*RALPH sits with a puzzled expression on his face and says nothing Impatiently, looks at Ralph*) Ralph (*RALPH still doesn't respond but looks as if he's pondering something*) Ralph!

PETE. Ralph, he's calling your name

RALPH I know I just don't know an appropriate response.

PETE Just say "here "

RALPH Are you sure that's appropriate?

PETE (*Sternly*) Say "here," Ralph

RALPH. (*Quickly obeying*) Here Ralph.

PETE Close enough.

DAN. Terry

TERRY. Yo.

DAN. Chris.

CHRIS. (*Bored*) Here.

DAN. Fred

FRED I object.

PETE. You can't object.

FRED. I can if I want. In Parliamentary Procedure I'm allowed. I saw it on TV.

PETE. But we're just taking roll. You can't object to your own name.

FRED. Oh. (*Pauses*) Can I object later?

PETE. (*Appeasing him*) Yes, Fred, you can object whenever you like.

DAN. Jim.

JIM. Uh huh.

DAN. That's it. Everyone's present and accounted for.

PETE. We're all agreed we're here then.

FRED. *Now* I object.

PETE. You object to *what*?

FRED. (*Pauses, embarrassed*) To . . . ah . . . that the roll wasn't taken alphabetically.

PETE. Then make a motion.

FRED. (*Shocked*) You want me to do *what*?

PETE. Make a motion. Stand up and say that you want to make roll call alphabetical.

FRED. (*Stands sheepishly*) I want to make roll call alphabetical.

PETE. No. Say "I move that we make roll call alphabetical."

FRED. I move that we make roll call alphabetical.

PETE. Anyone second that motion? (*No one reacts*) Anybody?

CHRIS. I'll second it if he'll just sit down and let us get on with this thing. I've got homework to do! (*FRED sits down frowning*)

PETE. We have a second. All in favor say "Aye."

EVERYONE. (*But FRED*) Aye.

PETE. Opposed say "Nay."

FRED. Nay. (*Everyone grumbles and gripes about this*)

PETE. Fred! You can't be opposed to your own motion!

FRED. I changed my mind.

PETE. (*Upset*) Aw, come on, cut it out, will you? (*To Dan*) Strike all that from the record.

DAN. After I just got done writing it all down? No way!

PETE. Never mind. Fred was outvoted anyway. Let's go on to Old Business.

TERRY. What old business? This is our first meeting!

PETE. Fine. No old business? Then let's handle new business.

TERRY. I think we should discuss church doctrine.

PETE. Wait.

JIM. No, we need to elect a Pastor first.

TERRY. We can't have a Pastor if we don't know what to believe!

JIM. But a Pastor will help us decide what to believe.

TERRY. First a doctrine!

JIM. No! A Pastor! (*TERRY and JIM stand and begin arguing, then yelling at each other. PETE tries to interrupt*)

PETE. Hey, one at a time. (*No response*) Guys . . . Jim . . . Terry . . . Hey! (*Still no response. Finally he pulls out a referee's whistle and blows it. JIM and TERRY freeze and look at Pete*) Time out! Go back to your corners, wait for the bell to ring then come out with your gloves up!

FRED. I object.

PETE. Will you quit objecting! You don't even know what you're objecting to!

FRED. I don't care. Whatever it is, I'm objecting to it.

RALPH. I think we should put a candy machine in the church lobby.

PETE. That's out of order.

RALPH. Already? We haven't even gotten it yet!

DAN (*Hunched over his pad trying to write everything down*) Could you all talk slower? I'm getting a handcramp.

CHRIS I'm gonna fail my test tomorrow.

PETE (*Wiping forehead from exasperation, sighs*) Okay . Terry had the floor first (*Everyone lifts their feet and looks down at the floor*) It's just an expression

TERRY (*Stands*) Thank you As I said, we need to develop church doctrine

JIM. Why?

TERRY Because

JIM Because why?

TERRY. 'Cause I said so!

PETE Will you two stop it' (*Pause*) I think we need to discuss this point I submit to you that as a new church trying to avoid the mistakes of other churches and our elders, we shouldn't do *anything* about doctrine

TERRY What?!?

PETE Remember a couple of years ago when our church was going to split? What were they going to split over' Doctrine Why can't our doctrine be to just love Jesus and love each other? Then we'll have nothing to split over Right?

TERRY. (*Thinking about it*) I don't know about that.

JIM I think that makes sense. What has split churches, caused wars (*Stands*) and resulted in mass killings throughout the centuries' Difference in doctrine' (*Quickly*) Now lets vote for a Pastor.

TERRY. Wo! Not so fast' I think we need to talk about this more.

JIM What's to talk about? Let's love Christ and each other. Period.

TERRY. I think –

JIM. It's simpler this way! Now let's vote for a Pastor.

TERRY. Hold it! We're talking about doctrine!

JIM. It's a closed issue! We've decided to love each other, you idiot!

TERRY. Don't call me an idiot, you jerk!

PETE. (*Blows whistle again*) Listen to yourselves! You're ready to split us up deciding over the doctrine about church doctrine!

CHRIS. Why do we have to decide *now*? Why can't we just make it up as we go along? I have to go home, I have—

EVERYONE. Homework to do.

PETE. We know. But that's a good idea. All in favor of discussing church doctrine later say "aye."

EVERYONE. Aye.

PETE. Oppposed? (*Everyone looks at Fred*)

FRED. What are you looking at *me* for?

PETE. Did you get all that, Dan?

DAN. (*Writing*) Yeah. I think so.

PETE. Read it back just to be sure.

DAN. Well, as best as I can figure, we've decided not to decide on our position on church doctrine until we make it up later on. In other words, we're agreed we don't agree on what we believe since we don't know what it is we believe until we agree on it later.

PETE. Right! (*Pauses confused*) I think.

JIM. Now let's choose a Pastor. (*Slowly stands as he clears throat with false humility*) I think we need someone with dedication and experience. (*Chuckles*) I just happen to have been class president at school for three years and—

RALPH. I nominate Pete for Pastor.

TERRY. I second that. (*Stands quickly*) All in favor say "aye."

EVERYONE. (*But Pete and Jim*) Aye.

TERRY. Opposed?

JIM. What about me?

RALPH. You can be minister of youth and music.

JIM. But we're *all* youth and there is no music!

RALPH. Then I guess you're out of a job. (*To Pete*) Can the next order of business be to serve snacks at these meetings? I'm hungry.

PETE. Look, I'm flattered about all this but are you *sure* you want *me* to be Pastor?

TERRY. No. But you'll do a better job than Jim. Besides, you're the one who got us involved in this mess in the first place.

PETE. Well, gee guys, I'm honored that you would bestow such faith in me and let me say right now that ..

CHRIS. I move we quit now.

PETE. (*Continuing*). . . I will take this . . .

JIM. Second

PETE. (*Continuing*) very seriously and . . . ah, well, all in favor say "Aye."

EVERYONE. Aye.

PETE. Opposed? (*Silence*) That's it. I'll call everyone about what we do next. (*Everyone rushes out except DAN. PETE sits down looking thoughtfully*)

DAN. (*Approaching him slowly after all have gone*) What do you think?

PETE. (*Enthusiastically*) I think it's great! We're going to be the *best* church ever! The way a church *should* be. I've got some good ideas for programs and stuff. I can't wait to get started. Tomorrow night we'll start visiting area homes to get new members! I'll call everyone to let them know.

DAN. (*Doubtfully*) Whatever you say . . . (*Speaks as if trying the name on for size*) Pastor. (*He pats him on the back and exits)*

PETE. (*Dreamily*) Pastor. (*He slowly stands and moves down center. The lights fade—or curtain closes—behind him. Spot focuses on him alone. In a press conference-style, various voices from the audience begin asking him questions . . .)*

VOICE 1. Pastor, what are your immediate plans?

PETE. I believe firstly in the reaffirmation of those things which we first believed!

VOICE 1. Meaning what?

PETE. Exactly. (*Looks around as hands are raised and various voices call out "Pastor, Pastor" to get his attention. He points to Voice 2*) Yes, I see that hand. (*VOICE 2 stands*)

VOICE 2. With current issues, what will be your stand?

PETE. Probably the pulpit. Or a box until we can afford one. (*Hands are raised, points to Voice 1 again*)

VOICE 1. (*Stands*) Back to my original question, sir.

PETE. Go right ahead. (*Points to Voice 3*) I saw your hand.

VOICE 3. What is your doctrine on sprinkling?

PETE. If the lawn needs it, I'm all for it. First we have to get a lawn. (*More hands, points to Voice 4*) You're on.

VOICE 4. (*Stands*) Do you believe in predestination as outlined by Calvin or do you hold to a free will doctrine?

PETE. That's a *very* good question. (*Looking around*) Are there any more good questions? (*More hands, points to Voice 2*) Uh huh.

VOICE 2. Based on your studies, do you believe in a pre-trib, mid-trib or post-trib rapture.

PETE. (*Pauses*) Yes. (*Points to Voice 1*) Go on.

VOICE 1. About my original question . . .

PETE. Oh yes! I'm glad you brought that up because

it is currently under scrutiny by our committee for authority delegation which handed the problem over to our subcommittee on deliberation and subcategorization restrictions. We should have an answer within 30 days or your money back. (*Hands up, points to Voice 3*) Yes.

VOICE 3. Will your church have a dress code?

PETE   No. We'll probably do it in plain English (*Points to Voice 4*) Yep.

VOICE 4   How do you feel about Arab-Israeli relations?

PETE   I don't have any now but I don't think I'd hold it against them if they married into my family. Well, that's all the time I have for questions . . . (*All the voices stand up and cry out "Pastor!" As they do this, lights [and curtain] come up on Pete's garage where LESLIE enters and calls "Pastor " Frustrated, she screams it one more time, silencing the voices in the audience who sit down*) Pastor!

PETE. (*Snapping out of his dream*) What!?! (*Turns to her, startled*) Oh, hi, Leslie.

LESLIE. You must have been daydreaming. Congratulations on being voted as Pastor last night.

PETE   Thank you

LESLIE. Now that we're moving seriously with this church experiment, I think we should consider someone to lead the choir, don't you?

PETE. Well, I–

LESLIE. I know you'll want someone qualified and I (*Fishes in purse*) just happen to have a song I wrote. (*Pulls out sheet music looks around the room*) Hmmm, no piano. That's all right, I can do it without.

PETE. I really don't think–

LESLIE.   Listen to this . . . (*She tries to sing Opera-style except she has no voice quality, tone, key, pitch or tune*)

I love to sing Amazing Grace

It puts a smile upon my face
And on that hill so far away
I wish—

PETE. (*Winces*) Leslie . . .

LESLIE. It moves you, doesn't it? My mother used to say I have a voice that can do amazing things

PETE. Like strip paint off of cars Y'know, I think— (*ANN enters stage right*)

ANN. Yoo hoo! Pastor Peter! (*Stops in her tracks, speaks sourly*) Oh, Leslie.

LESLIE. (*Snobbishly*) Ann.

ANN I just happened to be in the neighborhood and thought—

LESLIE. You're too late, Annie dear, *I'm* going to direct choir.

ANN. *You?* (*Chuckles, looks to Pete*) I think you should have your ears checked, Pastor

PETE Wait a minute—

LESLIE. I suppose you thought *you* should do it?

ANN. I assumed they wanted someone with *talent*, but since *you're* doing it, I guess not.

LESLIE. Are you implying that—

ANN No implication to it, Leslie.

PETE. Girls—

ANN. When it comes to your singing you are —how do they say?—a brick short of a load

LESLIE. I can outsing you anyday!

ANN Ha! (*LESLIE begins singing "Amazing Grace". To retaliate, ANN begins singing "A Mighty Fortress Is Our God". Louder and louder they both sing with each line until they're both virtually screaming the songs at each other*)

PETE. Girls . . . (*Pauses*) Girls . . . (*Another pause*)

Leslie, Ann . . (*Yells*) Hey! (*Both stop singing and look at him*) I think Jim is going to direct music. (*Both look at him shocked*)

LESLIE. Jim?

PETE. (*Nods*) Yes.

ANN. I'd rather have Leslie than Jim!

LESLIE. Jim?

ANN. (*Turning her nose up*) Well! (*Grabs Leslie's arm*) Come on, I don't think we should have any part of this! (*They walk stage right*)

LESLIE. You're right, Ann. I thought from the start this church idea was *stupid* (*They exit PETE sits down with exasperation as MARY enters stage left. Seeing him, she suddenly decides to sneak up behind and put her hands over both his eyes*)

MARY. Guess who.

PETE. Jim's choir director so just forget it.

MARY. Wrong. Guess again.

PETE. (*Thinking*) Ummmm . . . Santa Claus.

MARY. Nope.

PETE. The Easter Bunny.

MARY. No!

PETE I need a hint. Are you man, animal or vegetable?

MARY. Yes.

PETE. Bigger than a breadbox?

MARY. (*Looking herself over with chagrin*) Usually.

PETE. Smaller than the Empire State Building?

MARY. Only on weekends.

PETE. I give up.

MARY. It's the girl you said you'd take to lunch.

PETE. Which one?

MARY. (*Slaps him*) As Pastor you should be all-knowing. (*She moves to his side*) Where do you want to go?

PETE (*Frowns*) I'm sorry, Mary, but I can't. Fred called and said that there was something urgent he had to talk to be about. He should be here any minute.

MARY. See? I *told* you this is how it would be.

PETE. I'm sorry. It'll happen just this once. Never again.

MARY. You're wrong. It'll happen over and over again. (*Sighs*) I'm not up for this, Pete. I told you I don't want to be a Pastor's girlfriend.

PETE. What do you want me to do? I can't quit. Who else is there to do it?

MARY. I don't know and I don't care. (*Heads stage left to exit but turns back to him and speaks sarcastically*) Call me when you have the *time*, Pastor. (*She exits*)

PETE. (*Turning and speaking to no one*) And that's three (*FRED enters Stage Left, he is eating an apple and wearing a baseball cap*)

FRED. Wow, Mary almost knocked me over. Is she mad?

PETE. A little.

FRED. I guess she heard about you and Leslie, huh?

PETE. Me and *who*!?!?! (*He gapes with wide eyes*)

FRED Someone saw her here earlier today. Y'know, as Pastor you should be more careful. People are watching you closer than ever now.

PETE. (*Speechless*) But, but—

FRED. I suppose everybody knows about it by now. That could hurt you, good buddy. (*He puts his half-eaten apple down on the table. PETE moans and drops his head into his arms on the table*) That isn't what I came to talk to you about, though. I was thinking about a very important outreach for our new church that's guaranteed to bring in lost souls.

PETE   (*Lifts up head*) What's that, Fred?

FRED   (*Sits down*) Sports We need to develop sports leagues and activities

PETE   Is *that* the urgent thing you wanted to talk to me about?

FRED   I know you'd think so, too The way I got it laid out is we have Bowling on Monday nights Softball practice on Tuesday nights Volleyball on Wednesday Basketball on Thursdays Friday nights we can have miniature golf or football when it's in season And Saturday – the softball games

PETE   What about visitation – or all the other programs, for that matter?

FRED   Let the women do it! That's what they're around here for anyway.

PETE. (*Wincing*) Somehow I don't think they'll see it that way

FRED   Big deal As Pastor you need to show authority.

PETE   (*Trying to be patient, clears throat*) Fred, I think we should put all this on hold for now. Maybe after the church is settled, we –

FRED   (*Childishly*) Aww   I *knew* you'd be a wimp about it. (*Stands up*) Well .   I *object*!

PETE   This isn't a business meeting. You can't object.

FRED   I do anyway! Sports is an important ministry!

PETE   Not everyone thinks so.

FRED. Women and wimps!

PETE. (*Trying to be reasonable*) But, Fred –

FRED. (*Stubbornly*) I object (*Quickly speaking as he stands and heads Stage Left*) Object, object, object! And I hope you and Leslie don't work out! (*As he exits*) I object!

PETE. (*Sighs*) Four. I must be on some sort of winning streak. (*RALPH peeks his head, then full body stage left sheepishly)*

RALPH. Pastor?

PETE *(Mimicking the same sheepish voice)* Whator? *(He does this without turning to face the speaker, RALPH signals to someone offstage but they won't enter, he signals more forcefully, slowly WALLY comes on)*

RALPH I brought a new member for you to meet

PETE *(Turns to see Wally, stands up and looks at him curiously)* Hello *(Moves slowly towards Wally with hand outstretched to shake)* I'm   *(Changes mind upon looking more closely at Wally and lets hand drop)*   Pete *(Looks puzzled at Ralph)* Ralph?

RALPH This is Wally. I found him sleeping in an alley downtown

PETE I see .   ah, Wally, (?), would you wait right there a moment? *(He grabs Ralph and drags him down center with their backs to everything else on stage)*

RALPH What's wrong?

PETE Why did you bring him here? *(As they converse, WALLY sees the half-eaten apple on the table, quietly walks over to it, sits down and begins eating it)*

RALPH. Aren't we supposed to help the poor and needy?

PETE Well, yes But we need to get established first I can't keep him here

RALPH Can't you at least talk to him? Maybe you can tell him a little bit about what we're doing He seemed very interested when I told him in the alley

PETE What were you doing in an alley?

RALPH It was a short-cut home. I tripped over him

PETE How did you do that?

RALPH. He was buried under a bunch of papers and garbage. I thought he was dead.

PETE He smells like it. *(Thinks)* I suppose I could talk

to him. (*He puts on his fake smile and turns toward Stage Left*) Well, Wally . . . (*Both PETE and RALPH look puzzled until they turn and see him sitting at the table, PETE walks over and sits down, RALPH stays at a distance*) So tell me about yourself.

WALLY. I'm hungry Got anything to eat?

PETE. (*To Ralph*) I can see why you two are friends. (*To Wally*) When was the last time you had anything to eat?

WALLY. (*Squints an eye, looks upward in thought*) August . . (*Pauses*) . . . 1980.

PETE That's impossible

WALLY. You're right. Maybe it was November. (*To Ralph*) I thought you said we were going to eat!

RALPH. (*Helplessly to Pete*) My parents would've killed me if I took him home.

PETE. (*Sighs*) You know where the kitchen is Just clean up your mess.

RALPH Come on, Wally. (*WALLY gets up, he and RALPH cross to Stage Right*)

PETE I'll be in as soon as I . . . (*Sniffs the air*) spray. (*WALLY and RALPH exit PETE stands, picks up some papers and begins fanning the air*) I don't suppose he would sleep in an alley that gets rained on. (*JIM enters stage left, sniffs the air and turns to leave again*)

JIM. I'll come back some other time.

PETE. Wait! Come on in, it should go away soon.

JIM. (*Walking in*) Did your sewers back up?

PETE No, we have . . . oh, never mind. What's up?

JIM. (*Pulling a piece of paper out of his back pocket*) I wanted to show you a list of songs for us to sing Sunday morning.

PETE. Oh good. (*Takes the list and reads it, face over-*

shadows with concern) These are the songs?

JIM. (*Proudly*) Yep.

PETE. "Somewhere Over The Rainbow"? "Wishing On A Four Leaf Clover"? (*Incredulous*) "As Time Goes By"?

JIM. Is something wrong?

PETE. But these songs aren't for church. What about "The Old Rugged Cross," "Amazing Grace," "How Great Thou Art" . . . songs like that?

JIM. We can't Those songs sing about *doctrine* and we don't have that yet. I thought *my* songs would be non-offensive.

PETE. (*Hands him the list*) We need to find Christian songs . . . songs about Christ.

JIM. But we *can't!* (*RALPH and WALLY enter Stage Right, both with armloads of food from the refrigerator*)

RALPH Thanks, Pastor. (*They're both walking extremely fast so that by the time PETE can react, they've exited Stage Left*)

PETE. (*Turns, panics*) Hey!

JIM. (*Grabbing him*) What songs do *you* think we should do?

PETE. (*In shock*) He cleaned me out! (*Sits down wearily*)

JIM. He cleaned me out? Sounds a little contemporary for a worship service. (*Grabs list from Pete's hand*) But I'll check on it. (*He exits Stage Left*)

PETE (*Sighs*) I wonder if the Apostles got started this way. (*Lights fade to BLACKOUT*)

Scene Three

*Lights (curtain) up on Pete's garage. It is later in the
evening and DAN, alone, is pacing, looking at watch
and pacing more He sits down, drums his fingers
on the table, looks at door, stands and paces again
Aimlessly, he wanders around the table to Pete's position and suddenly stops, pauses, looks around the
garage playfully with a mischievous expression on
his face. He straightens up authoritatively and, in
a style and timing reminiscent of Groucho Marx,
begins an imaginary business meeting .*

DAN. (*Picks up a nearby hammer and slams it on table
like a gavel*) Okay, meeting will now come to order. (*he
laughs at his own silliness then gets serious again clear-
ing his throat*) Mr. Minuteman, read the minutes. No
minutes? How about seconds? Thirds? Never mind. We
can't have it in thirds. Just divide it in half. All in favor
say "aye." (*Pounds hammer again*) Those in disfavor don't
matter anyway. Eyes have it Ears, nose and throat will
have to wait. Any old business? Any new business? No
business at all? No wonder we're going bankrupt. (*Pauses*)
As a bored President, I'd like to say how much I appreciate
your hard work and devotion. I'd *like* to. Just kidding. In
all honesty, I wouldn't be where I am now if I couldn't
step on each one of you along the way – I mean, unless

28

each one of you were with me every step of the way . .
(*PETE enters Stage Right. He is a mess — dirty, shirt-sleeves torn, tie is pulled asunder. he drags his feet as he walks, panting out of breath DAN is embarrassed that he was caught in his charade .   .*)

PETE. I need to sit down.

DAN. (*Surprised, embarrassed*) Pete! I was just . . . (*Sees how messy he is, speaks with concern*) What happened to you? I thought we were supposed to meet here at eight o'clock for visitation.

PETE. *Seven* o'clock We were supposed to meet at *seven* o'clock When nobody showed up, I decided to go by myself

DAN. So what happened? How in the world did you get so dirty?

PETE Well, one guy set his dogs on me and I fell down a hill trying to get away.

DAN Is that how you tore your shirt?

PETE. Huh? (*Realizing, he puts his hand up to the tear*) Oh, that. It must be from the motorcycle gang.

DAN Motorcycle gang!!

PETE They called themselves "The Devil's Psychos." Good name. One guy tore my Bible in half with his bare hands

DAN Really?

PETE And then he tried to shove it up my nose (*Rubs nose*) I'll be sneezing scripture verses for weeks

DAN. Wow

PETE. See these scratches on my face?

DAN. They did that, too?

PETE No They're from a herd of Hare Krishnas I stumbled across. They started beating me with their flowers. Those roses have thorns! The only friendly face

I saw was a little old lady who invited me in and made me eat some brownies filled with coconut, pineapple . . .

DAN. That's not so bad.

PETE. . . . garlic and onions in them. See? (*Breathes at him*)

DAN. (*Waves hand from the smell*) Yeah.

PETE. (*Groans, holds stomach*) I think I have food poisoning.

DAN. Well, did you get anyone who'll come?

PETE. I had one guy on a street corner say he'd come if I gave him five dollars.

DAN. Did you?

PETE. I did after he pulled a knife on me But I don't think he'll be here Sunday (*Angrily*) What happened to everyone tonight?

DAN. I'm not sure. Chris had homework. Jim said he was too tired and Ralph said he had to stay home and watch his favorite TV show

PETE. A *TV* show!

DAN. "Bowling For Dollars." It's a rerun of his favorite episode. A $10,000 jackpot or something.

PETE. (*Stands angrily — sways — holds onto chair*) That's it. I want an emergency meeting with everyone. Tonight. Now.

DAN. I don't know if —

PETE. Just call them and tell them to get here right away. We can't have a church if no one's going to work for it. I can't do it myself Pastor or not

DAN But they might not want to come

PETE. Tell them we're going to work this whole thing out tonight or we won't do it all. (*DAN nods, begins moving to Stage Right as PETE slips down in the chair from exhaustion . . . the lights fade to BLACKOUT [curtain falls]*)

Scene Four

*Before the lights (or curtain) come up, obvious pande-
monium and arguing is going on. With the exception
of FRED (who quit earlier), we see everyone in the
same positions as in their meeting before. Lights
(curtain) come up on them standing and shouting at
each other. PETE, still dressed as he was in the last
scene, slowly takes out his whistle and blows it.
Everyone gets quiet and looks at him*

PETE. (*Wearily*) All right, I think we've gotten off
track. Dan, read back what—*exactly*—we're trying to
decide.

DAN. We're trying to decide whether our mop handles
will be blue or red

JIM. Red is a good Christian color.

TERRY. But blue is—

PETE. Hold it!

CHRIS. I'm gonna fail school, I just know it.

RALPH. Forget that! I missed the end to "Bowling For
Dollars"!

CHRIS. Big deal.

RALPH. It is!

PETE. That's the problem! Everyone keeps thinking of
themselves! (*Trying unsuccessfully to hold back his anger*)
No one'll think of what's good for everyone else. What's

31

good for the *church* Look at us! We're doing exactly what we were rebelling against' When we're not fighting about mop handles we're trying to beat each other out of positions or just plain apathetic about doing any work I almost got killed tonight trying to do alone what we *all* should have been doing (*Turns away from them and walks to Stage Left in silence Everyone looks at each other guiltily*) Either we're going to do this right or we won't do it at all (*Sighs after a moment of silence*) I would suggest that we pray together about this but it'll probably wind up a contest of who can pray the loudest (*Rubs his face with his hands*) It's late and we're all tired let's sleep on it and meet back here tomorrow (*Turns back to them*) I move we dismiss

JIM (*Quietly*) Second
PETE All in favor say "Aye "
EVERYONE Aye.
PETE Opposed. Fine. Goodnight (*Turns away from them and marches off Stage Right Everyone looks at each other guiltily and slowly gets up and files out Stage Left DAN, the last to leave, looks around the garage sadly and somberly walks off Lights fade to BLACKOUT Curtain falls*)

Scene Five

The next day Lights (curtain) up on Pete's garage It is empty DAN enters Stage Left, shakes his head at the empty room and sits down in his usual place PETE walks in briskly at first, sees that only Dan is there, slowly walks to his position at the table and remains standing

PETE. (*Stubbornly*) Take the roll, please.

DAN But, Pete . . .

PETE. (*More firmly*) Take the roll.

DAN. (*Humoring him, clears throat nervously*) Please give an appropriate response when your name is called . (*Pauses awkwardly*) Terry. (*Pause*) Chris. (*Pause*) Ralph (*Pause*) Jim. (*Pause*) Pete

PETE. Here

DAN And I am here (*PETE slowly sits down, defeated*)

PETE. I guess that's that. It was a failure

DAN (*Rises*) No, I don't think it was a *failure* (*Moves to seat next to Pete and sits down*) I think we learned some very valuable lessons.

PETE (*Doubtfully*) Yeah

DAN No, I mean it Stop and think about what you've been through the past couple of days I don't know about you but I think I've learned a lot

PETE Give me a hint.

DAN Well   I learned that it takes a lot of work and commitment to keep a church going And it's not just the Pastor's responsibility, *everyone* has to work at it

PETE. (*Nods*) Okay Go on

DAN And I think I learned that it can't be done without the love of Jesus Christ I don't mean the love we talked about and voted on but a *real* love that lets us love each other in spite of ourselves The way God has always loved us

PETE. (*Pauses, half-smiles and nods*) You got me on that one Keep talking

DAN And there'll never be such a thing as a perfect church as long as it's made up of imperfect people (*Pauses, looks at Pete*) How did I score?

PETE (*Stands*) You learn your lessons well. (*He slow-

ly walks Downstage Center) Yeah, you learned them well.
(*The lights dim and spot focuses on him alone as he looks
out above the audience)*

PASTOR. So what is your conclusion?

PETE. Well, Pastor, our church has a lot of problems.
But I guess every church does. The answer to those problems isn't to give up and leave but to join together in
unity of mind and heart . . . one spirit resolved to spread
the love of Jesus Christ among each other and to those
outside of us.

PASTOR. Then the experiment was a success.

PETE. (*Puzzled*) A success?

PASTOR For you to say what you just said . . . It was
a success. (*PETE ponders this for a second, then smiles)*

PETE. Thanks, Pastor. (*He turns and exits upstage into the darkness Lights fade to BLACKOUT. Curtain)*

–THE END–

The author of *The First Church of Pete's Garage*, Paul
McCusker, is fast becoming one of America's most popular
playwrights for Christian youth. His collection of witty
skits entitled *Sketches of Harvest* proved so enormously
popular that he followed with another, the highly ac-
claimed *Souvenirs*. Both collections are available through
Baker's Plays as is his *Home for Christmas*, a seasonal
one-act of heartrending power.

OTHER TITLES AVAILABLE FROM BAKER'S PLAYS

MASHED POTATOES AND DAVEY

Megan Orr

Comedy / 5m, 6f, plus extras / Multiple Settings

This year, in a stroke of good will, Mr. Masterson invites bus kid Davey Bryant over for Thanksgiving dinner. The Masterson kids are appalled; Davey, the biggest bully the kids at Faith Baptist Church have ever seen, is coming to eat at their house! Together, the four Masterson kids (and guests) hatch an anti-Davey campaign to get rid of the pest for good. To add to the mayhem, Mrs. Masterson has been doing a little inviting—and matchmaking—of her own; the new, single youth pastor, Pastor Brian, as well as Erin Thompson, a young widow, and her two daughters will also be joining the festivities. But with three of the four young girls madly in love with Pastor Brian, bringing the pair together may be easier said than done. With falling bowls of mashed potatoes, invisible dogs, turkey costumes, slingshots, and Pilgrims, one thing's for certain—it'll be a Thanksgiving no one will ever forget!